e Thing in the Sink

D0112085

The Thing in the Sink

FRIEDA HUGHES

Hodder
Children's
Books

a division of Hodder Headline Limited

99210

Chapter One

"But Peter," said Mrs Pitt-Smith, " I'm sure you can find *something* to bring in as a pet. It doesn't matter if it's only a beetle or a house mouse. The idea is to hear the pet essays and meet the animals at the same time. You do have until the last week of term."

"I'm going to write an essay about my rabbit," announced Megan, "then I can bring it in to show you all."

"I'm going to bring in my python," said Jonathan, "then I can feed Megan's rabbit to it." Mrs Pitt-Smith frowned at him.

When he got home Peter found his mother in the kitchen. "Mum," he said, "you know I've always wanted a dog?" His mother nodded. "Well, do you think we might get one before the holidays? We have to write an essay on our pets by the end of term, and it would be a great chance for us to get a dog. I could call it George."

"Peter, we never said you could have a pet," his mother pointed out. "I honestly don't think you're quite old enough to take the responsibility yet."

"How about a snake, then?"

His mother shuddered. "They need specially heated tanks," she said, "and you would have to feed it dead rats and mice."

"A mouse?" suggested Peter, getting desperate for *anything*.

"Definitely not."

"Oh," said Peter.

It looked as though it

was up to him to catch a beetle or
something. He would call it George.
Perhaps he could find a big, black one with
spikey feelers and feet that felt like velcro
against his skin.

A search of the garden
that afternoon turned
up two ants and a
large, curled-up dead spider.

What could he write about ants? They
have six legs, they're small, black and
squash easily. Peter looked down at the
two black smudges where the ants had
been flattened trying to get out of his
matchbox as he closed it, and decided that
ants were no good.

Chapter Two

That night Peter lay in the bath, trying to think how he could solve his problem.

His thoughts were interrupted by water gurgling in the overflow, and a squelching, shuffling, sucking sound.

"Mum!" cried Peter. "There's something wrong with the bath, the overflow is making funny noises."

"It's probably only the water settling," his mother called back.

Peter peered into the grill that covered the circular hole below the taps and blinked. An enormous eye blinked back.

"Mum, quick, come and have a look, there's definitely something in the overflow!" he shouted. His mother rushed in and peered into it. Then she smiled and sighed.

"Peter, really, you're seeing things. There's nothing there at all, it's just a hole into the pipe that carried the water away. Even a frog couldn't get in there."

"But I saw an eye," insisted Peter. "It blinked at me."

"Don't tell such stories," snapped his mother. "Are you teasing me just because I said you couldn't have a pet? It's not the way to do it, you know. It was probably just the reflection of your own eye in a water bubble." She left him alone to clean his teeth.

Peter turned on the sink tap, but there was something blocking the drain and the water wouldn't run away.

He turned the tap off and called for his mother again. "What is it *this* time?" she demanded.

Peter was bent over the sink looking into the drain. "The eye is here as well," he gasped, beckoning her over. "It's blocking the sink! Quick, come and have a look before it goes away again." As he finished speaking, the basin began to empty.

Reluctantly, his mother stared into the drain. Then she scowled at him, grunted, and walked out. The eye had disappeared.

Every day for the next two weeks Peter
went to school without knowing what he
was going to do about his pet essay. He had
even hidden bits of cheese all over the
house in the hope that he could attract a
mouse, or even a rat.

"Don't worry about it too much," Mrs
Pitt-Smith consoled him. "If you really
can't find anything, perhaps you could
share one of the other children's pets. Find
someone who will let you write about their
cat or their dog."

But Peter didn't want to write about the same animal as someone else. He wanted something different. Something of his *own*. Even better, he would like something really unusual like a lizard or a parrot.

Every night Peter peered into the drain of the sink in the bathroom, and stared into the blackness of the bath overflow, but the big, blinking eye wasn't there.

Chapter Three

In the kitchen one afternoon, Peter's
mother was sitting with her back to the
kitchen sink. Suddenly, something moving
behind her caught Peter's attention.

"Look, look at that!" he shouted. But his
mother was too slow. By the time she
turned around, the thing that Peter saw
had gone.

"It's not fair!" cried Peter, running to the sink and looking at the plug hole. "It really was here, honestly it was. It was the eye again, only this time it came out of the sink on the end of a long green stalk."

"I think you're making it all up," his mother said sternly. "There is no such thing as an eye in the sink, and certainly not one that pops out of the drain on a stalk as though it were a lollipop. I want you to go to bed. Now."

Peter crept upstairs.

When he woke in the morning there were water patches all over his bedroom carpet, spaced apart like footprints, but all the wrong shape. In fact, they had no real shape at all. He followed them. They led all the way down the hall and back to the bathroom.

Peter's mother caught him on the landing. "Oh Peter, you didn't dry your feet off when you bathed this morning," she scolded. Peter opened his mouth and was just about to say it wasn't him when he stopped himself. She wouldn't believe him, so what was the point?

In the bathroom, he locked the door and sat on the edge of the bath, studying the sink. "I know you're in there," he said, feeling rather foolish. He wondered if talking to the bathroom furniture was the first sign of madness.

There was no sound, no gurgle, no bubbling of water in the pipes. Peter put his face right into the sink. "I *know* you're in there!" he shouted.

"Peter, what are you doing?" cried his mother outside.

"Oh, er, nothing, Mum. I was just talking to myself."

"Well, could you talk to yourself so I can't hear you," she asked. Peter waited until she'd gone then he tried again.

"If you don't show yourself, you great big eye," he whispered, "I'll pour disinfectant down the plug hole, and just see how you like that!" Still nothing happened.

Peter picked up the disinfectant his mother used to clean out the bath and tilted it over the drain. He was bluffing, but the thing in the sink didn't know that.

A long-fingered green and brown hand suddenly shot up through the centre of the grill over the drain, and grabbed the bottle from Peter's hand. Peter struggled and tried to get the bottle back, but the hand threw it across the room, then disappeared back into the piping.

Peter was too frightened to try anything
else. He quickly mopped up the
disinfectant, put the bottle back where he
found it and left for school, looking over
his shoulder the whole time in case
something might be following him.

All morning he was silent. When Mrs Pitt-Smith asked what was wrong, he told her it was because he hadn't found a pet yet for his end of term essay.

"Don't fret, Peter," Mrs Pitt-Smith told him pleasantly. "Megan has agreed that you may share her rabbit."

"You can come round and see Susannah any time you like," said Megan generously.

Peter sank further beneath his desk. That was all he needed: to share a rabbit called Susannah, how undignified! There had to be something he could do to get a pet of his own.

Chapter Four

That night he was too scared to clean his teeth or wash.

"But I can tell you haven't washed," said his mother, dragging him to the bathroom by the wrist. "You have smudges from your painting class all over your hands and face."

She shut Peter in the bathroom and told him not to come out until he was spotless.

Peter stared at the sink and the bath as though they were about to come to life. Minutes passed.

"Are you going to stand there all night?" enquired a small voice suddenly.

"Where are you?" asked Peter looking around nervously. "And who are you?" He held his breath and waited.

"I'm in the bath," replied the voice, laughing. The green and brown scaly hand appeared through the overflow and waved at him.

"But I'm in the sink as well," said the voice, and the eye on a stalk appeared from the plughole and blinked. It was enormous, far too large to fit into the sink drain, so was the hand.

"How can you be in both places at once?" asked Peter in spite of the way his knees were trembling.

"Easy," said the little voice. "I stretch through the pipes. I could probably reach the kitchen sink with my right foot if I tried."

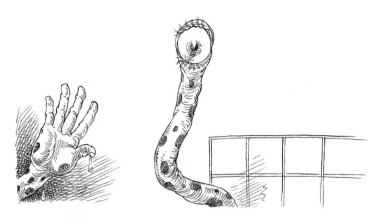

"They were *your* wet footprints on the landing last night, weren't they?" Peter accused.

"Guilty," said the voice. "I wanted to have a proper look at you. It's not often I get to see a whole person, usually I see only what is visible from whichever drain I'm in."

"Do you live in other people's drains as well?"

"Oh yes, I travel around the underground water system all the time. It would be dull to stay in one place for too long," replied the creature. "I can go anywhere water can go."

"Can I see you properly?" asked Peter, his courage returning rapidly now the thing in the sink was actually talking to him. "After all, you've seen me."

The eye disappeared back into the drain with a sucking sound, and the hand stretched out further from the bath overflow.

It stretched and stretched and behind it came a squeezed, elongated body with a face distorted in its length. It oozed from a hole in the overflow grill like green and brown toothpaste, until it was all there, coiled up like a long, thin green and brown snake in the bottom of the bath.

The shapeless heap stood up and began
to pat itself into a more solid mass.

"Can you be any shape you like?" asked
Peter.

"Oh yes," replied the creature, blinking
at him with its enormous eyes. "Any shape
at all. What would you like me to be?"
There was a hiss of escaping air and the
blob contorted itself into the shape of a
large toad. The toad grinned.

There was another hissing noise and the toad became a large boat, rocking in the bottom of the bath.

"That's fantastic!" cried Peter. "But what shape are you really?"

The result was something like a large potato with claw-like hands and feet and eyes that stared out from the upper part of its blobby body above a wide, lipless mouth. It stood no higher than Peter's shoulder.

"Just wait until Mum sees you!" cried Peter, clapping his hands. "She'll have to believe me now."

"Ah, no, can't be done, I'm afraid," said the creature spreading out its huge hands. "You know what adults are like, they'd want to put me in a zoo where scientists would examine me. They'd poke me and prod me and laugh at me. If you tell anyone about me, I'll just have to leave."

One thing was for certain, Peter didn't want the blob to leave.

"Where did you come from?" he asked curiously. "Do you have parents?"

"No idea," replied the blob stepping out of the bath. "One day I woke up and I just was. I've never met anyone else quite like me, Peter. Oh yes, and you can call me George if you like." George reached out a slimy hand and took Peter's in his enormous fingers. "How do you do."

"You've been eavesdropping on all our conversations!" cried Peter accusingly. "You know I want a pet called George!" He was sure George's top part blushed slightly.

Peter smuggled George into his room
and they talked all night. George had never
enjoyed himself so much in his life. Never
before had he actually dared to try and
make friends with anyone. Now he could
play records, read books, use Peter's train
set and talk to someone else instead of
himself.

Peter gave him a towel to sit on because
water constantly oozed from the pores of
his skin, and dripped off the ends of his
fingers and toes.

"You seem very happy this morning," said Peter's mother. Peter grinned at her. George was sleeping under his bed with a cold water bottle in case he need a bit of moisture.

"No more 'eye' sightings?" asked his mother. Peter shook his head.

"You were right, Mum, it must have been my imagination," he told her. She positively beamed with relief.

Chapter Five

It was the last Monday of term and
everyone had brought in their essays and
pets, or an animal they were able to borrow
from a friend or relative. Megan had her
big, white, pink-eyed rabbit. Jonathan had
been as good as his word and carried his
python around his neck so no one would
go near him. Others had brought dogs on
leads, cats in carry baskets, mice in wire
cages, a tortoise, a garden spider with an
enormous patterned body and a duck on
the end of a dog leash.

Everyone wanted to know what Peter had written about and where his pet was, but he wouldn' tell them.

"That's because you don't really have anything to write about!" accused Jonathan.

At last, it was his turn to stand up in front of the class and read what he'd written about his pet. He looked right at Mrs Pitt-Smith and hoped she was going to like what he'd done.

"My essay is called 'George'," he told the class. "It's about my pet pig."

"But I haven't seen you bring in any pig," said Mrs Pitt-Smith. "Besides, pigs are the kind of animal that you only find on farms, and there isn't a farm for miles."

Peter whistled and there was a scratching at the door. The door swung open and in trotted a very fat green and brown pig, wagging its stringy tail.

"Pigs can't open doors," announced
Jonathan. "How did he do it?"

"My pig is an unusual pig," read Peter
from his essay. "He is so well-trained that
it is easy to keep him round the house, and
if he needs to go out, he can open the doors
himself. His favourite hobby is watching
television. His favourite food is ice cream."
The pig grunted in delight at the thought of
ice cream.

"He's still not as intelligent as a dog,"
cried one of the other boys, who was
holding a large droopy-eared mongrel on
the end of a well-chewed lead.

"He's so intelligent," Peter continued,
"that he even takes my dog for a walk."

"So where's your dog then?" demanded
Jonathan, who had really wanted to steal
the show with his python.

"Go and get the dog, George," instructed Peter. Piggy George, who had been sitting obediently at Peter's feet, trotted out of the room. There was a bark, and in came a dog. A big green and brown dog with massive shoulders and huge ears. It padded across the floor to Peter's feet and lay down with its head on its enormous paws. Peter patted it.

"Is there any more to your essay, Peter?" asked Mrs Pitt-Smith, eyeing the dog with mistrust.

"Oh yes, Miss," grinned Peter.

"You still haven't got anything as unusual as my python," snapped Jonathan.

The green and brown dog padded quietly out of the room.

A moment later, there was a dragging, sliding, scraping noise, and an enormous green and brown lizard pulled itself through the doorway on short, fat legs. Its long tongue flickered in and out of its mouth like a whip.

All the children screamed and stood on their chairs. "It's all right," shouted Peter, "it's completely harmless."

"I'm afraid I didn't include the lizard in my essay," he told Mrs Pitt-Smith apologetically.

"I don't suppose you have a rabbit as well, do you?" asked Megan. Peter quickly checked his essay.

"Actually, I do," he smiled. "Go get the rabbit," he told the lizard.

The lizard slid out of the door and a rabbit hopped back in. An enormous, slightly damp green and brown rabbit. Megan gasped. "Oooh," she cried, "can I stroke it?" Peter nodded. Megan cuddled the rabbit, and the rabbit began to purr. Peter frowned and the purring stopped.

"I think you must have an astonishingly patient mother," commented Mrs Pitt-Smith, "to put up with all the animals you've collected."

Grinning, Peter finished reading his essay.

Mrs Pitt-Smith was looking out of the staff room window as the children left at the end of the day. Walking out of the school gate was Peter, hand in hand with a baby dinosaur.

She blinked, and suddenly, Peter was walking out of the school gates arm in arm with his giant rabbit. The rabbit stopped for a moment, turned, looked straight at Mrs Pitt-Smith and gave an elegant bow.

"Humph," said Mrs Pitt-Smith, "strange animals they are breeding these days. Such peculiar colours . . . but nice manners."

HODDER

These colour story books are short, accessible
novels for newly confident readers

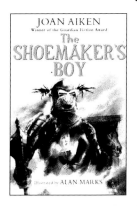

JOAN AIKEN
Winner of the Guardian Fiction Award
The
SHOEMAKER'S
BOY

Illustrated by ALAN MARKS

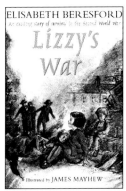

ELISABETH BERESFORD
An exciting story of survival in the Second World War
Lizzy's
War

Illustrated by JAMES MAYHEW

ELISABETH BERESFORD
the exciting sequel to Lizzy's War
Lizzy
Fights On

Illustrated by JAMES MAYHEW

LEON GARFIELD
Winner of the Whitbread Children's Book Award
Fair's
Fair

Illustrated by BRIAN HOSKIN

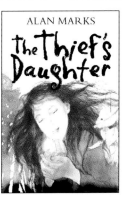

ALAN MARKS
the Thief's
Daughter

MICHAEL MORPURGO
Winner of the Smarties Prize
THE KING IN
THE FOREST

Illustrated by TONY KERINS

JILL PATON WALSH
By the Smarties prize-winning author of Thomas and the Tinners
Birdy and the
Ghosties

Illustrated by ALAN MARKS

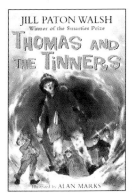

JILL PATON WALSH
Winner of the Smarties Prize
THOMAS AND
THE TINNERS

Illustrated by ALAN MARKS